IN THE
DRO

OM

Heitham Al-Sayed

Published in Oxford by The Onslaught Press
11 Ridley Road, OX4 2QJ
27 February 2017

ISBN: **978-1-912111-65-7**

Typeset in Jean François Porchez's **Le Monde Livre** &
Le Monde Sans inside, with Akira Kobayashi's **Din Next** on
the cover and title page

Designed & edited by **Mathew Staunton**

Printed & bound by Lightning Source

for Anastasiya

X-Time

a preface by Timothy Morton

What in the blazes . . . I mean what in the name of our Lord . . . I mean, Jesus H Christ on a stick. Are you sure you want to read this? Really sure? Are you wearing nylon underwear? It disintegrates at high speeds. There's no need to carry on you know. You could buy a sandwich and just walk away. Go on, just close this and walk quietly away. That's the best policy.

The thing is, in this ecological age of ours, the main message is: *we are already dead*. We are already dead, because our ideas about who we are and what kind of mission we're on have evaporated. Even US shock jock Rush Limbaugh's hand knows to care enough about his bald head to smear sunscreen on it to prevent the worst of global warming from turning him even redder.

It's actually a great relief to realize that you are dead. Trying not to die has become a thing of the past. You can exit from survival mode. Survival mode tends to be fatal in the long run, especially to the lifeforms around you.

This book contains sentences whose subject changes as they proceed. The nouveau roman was a powerful attempt at such a feat. Every few hours he felt a slight sinking sensation. It started at the pit of his stomach and would descend a little, not enough to pass entirely out of him, just a little soft collapse. There was never a moment when you were reading this, you reflected, when you felt balanced. Integrated. Like all the plot lines could be held in a tight little bundle like those bundles of sticks she saw decorating monuments in Rome. That was a lovely café in its day, the smokers in the twilight. Now the preface went all fucked up and strange, and she began to realize that this was a cheap imitation of the narrative itself, or possibly a cancerous metastasis of its cancerous metastasis, too much life, too many temporal layers.

Too many temporalities, too many inter-secting slices of time, the pastry that oozes out of telephones, nuclear submarines floating silent through Arctic waters, convex mirrors of gravity bending galaxies around a black hole, the way her eyes were so precisely shaped and how his crossed with hers, locked, zoom, pull, focus, zoom, pull. Sometimes truth comes in the form of flickering error and you have a devil of a time. I mean he had a devil of a time distinguishing between true and false, not because true was a lie, but because it wasn't, or because it might not be. If everything was a lie you'd know, and that would be true, so one thing wouldn't be a lie, so that *everything was a lie* was a lie.

One of those great French people, I think it was Jacques Lacan, said, *What constitutes pretense is that, in the end, you don't know whether it's pretense or not*. If you knew, reasoned the physicist, you would be able to discriminate true from false, so lying would be impossible. You can lie, he realized, because the true-false distinction is shimmering. It's not that everything is a lie. It's that being deceived is a possibility condition for truth, just like listening is the possibility condition for music, just like visualization is the basis of imagery, say of the grey smell of dust after rain, which I think is called *petrichor*. The dance of tiny flakes of stone in the air, after the bombing raid.

Zoom, click, focus, pull, the forest path expanding and staying still at the same time, spacetime breathing, its lungs heaving up and down, perhaps it's only trying to breathe, aka failing to breathe, and this could be the moment when the brain says, Shit, he's dying, dump the DMT: *Start the procedure*. The oxygen bag inflating and deflating by the hospital bed, a silicon swim bladder, how a fish breathed out of water for fifteen seconds, three hundred and seventy million years ago. An X-Fish. A fish with a mutant power, haunted by a spectral salamander-to-come, a futural penumbra like a grey astral halo shaped like one of those space vaginas that surround the saints in medieval paintings. Lifeforms are all ghosted by some X power like that, he said, lifeforms aren't ever exactly what they say they are on the can, they are slinkies made of time, metal helixes that tumble downstairs when you give them a pull, they stretch beyond their essential nature and

flop downwards, out of the water, collapsing
in the mud, heaving, gasping for breath,
here comes the wave, thank fuck I can
breathe again, what was *that*.

Time is the appearance that haunts a thing,
a spectral shadow cast by its difference
from itself, the reason why it exists at all.

All novels are haunted by this kind of
sentence, they said, as they examined the
suicide note in the autopsy room. It's as if
trying to tell a straightforward story is just
one kind of perverse pathway through a
possibility space of mutant time, spreading,
fanning outwards from cigars, dirty bollards
near to Wimbledon Chase train station,
that samosa he ate in 1987 still makes him
cringe. The fanning out of time like one of
those gigantic wafers in a gelato, a shell, a
fan, a flower are maps of silently executing
algorithms unfolding in three dimensions.
Cancerous outgrowths of recipes for sexual
display.

I'm ever so sorry about this.
But you're already in.

In the Droom

a novel by Heitham Al-Sayed

It is an inconvenience to be here but I don't mind.

It's been a few days since I lost him, and I know I should start looking. I know I was on the train that day and on the corner of the street in the north of the city because when I'm feeling weak I find it hard to give bad news, and I did feel weak. In fact I almost collapsed. He should have known that before, of course. I nearly stepped out in front of a car, I felt its breath brush past me and move my hair, the black metal and glass so near my teeth and my tongue.

I've been back but if he's not there I usually return later. It's worth checking. It's nearly sunset now and there's no point in staying here. Maybe I will go back to the station. He often passes through there.

Yesterday seems a very long time ago now but it can only be yesterday. It will be easy to check in a moment. In fact, I check all the time and it seems the clock has stopped in its ticking and mine always says the same number. It says it is the afternoon but it's clearly night outside, the orange street lights are filling up the room. I used to hate that light and how it bleached out all the colours and all the cars. Now I like the glow—it seems warm in the snow with no mountains.

I checked at the crossroads by the Grand Rex at midday on a beautiful early July day in the Paris sun. People and cars move in a languid resigned rhythm, the people average in their beauty. One has no desire to know more of them. They contain no mystery. How could they? They have all fed from the same pot.

I do remember how embarrassing it was for them. Their son soiled himself on the way home that day and never forgot it. I suppose he was sick or troubled in some way because it only ever happened once. He was quite a sickly child, but always full of life and energy. He hardly ever suffered from colds but seemed to spend a lot of his time with some exotic ailment or other. What a beautiful boy. I wonder what happened to him.

I spend a lot of time looking in that Spanish bar in town with the hexagon tiles on the ceiling and the juke box, but so far he has never come. I never understood who chose those songs. They were so good they would all become your favourite, and as they were the only ones on there, they had to be good. You would hear them a lot, that's for certain. The two brothers behind the bar. The benevolent old wrestler, a giant with white hair, benign and powerful and so calm. He knew the numbers of all the songs. He would help you. It was the same place but he loved being there. His dignity was a white in his hair. His dark-haired brother was a wall and an ugly one at that. Nothing came from him but bitter exclamations, declamations and orders. He hated being there. Why was the angry one ugly? What a stupid cliché, but which came first?

Everyone there was drunk and always stayed till the end when, finally, the lady would start mopping up and the bar would smell of bleach and change the taste of the drinks, but before we could finish our pints the door would open and people would start trickling in because it was time to open. I only ever got up to go to the toilets and always kept my seat by that little table video game which had never functioned as anything other than a table. So I was in there for a long time.

On the school bus the vinyl seats were hot and that's why I wasn't comfortable and preferred to walk. The smell of them was terrible in the sun.

My aunt's voice very slow in my ear as
I fall asleep, because I had a fever.

I hated shopping then. Supermarkets
and all the plastic and unripe fruit with
no taste and the light and always more
feeding and buying. Nowadays, I like it.
I take my time and enjoy it. The most
exhilarating experience is entering a
supermarket in another country for
the first time and not knowing, not
recognizing. It seems to me that that is
what they're really for. Magical packages,
parcels covered in a script unknown
until you learn the meanings and they're
really just chocolate biscuits but good
ones nevertheless.

One inconvenience is the sheer beauty
of falling in on oneself and folding
forward. The rolling sensation can be
distracting. It took days for me to get
used to it

I think I live in the mountains, but they must be the mountains of a city because even though there is snow outside the window, very deep, and a crow dipping down across the puffy white field, there is steam coming out of a vent on the dry cleaners below the cottage which is on the third floor above the bank. There are sheepfold sheep with little mists coming from their nostrils where there are cars in that crossroads just outside with the little mists coming from the exhausts. I can see the name by the bell but the letters change as I read across. I have spent many hours trying to read it but they are neither words nor letters made of numbers.

I'm sure if I could reach him I could warn him. There's nothing left in here so I can go inside when I like. He has surely left. But his name is still under the bell, on the black metal landing behind those shops in the mountains, far away from any other humans. I think he may be a woman.

IN THE GRAND HOUSE OF GOD YOU WILL FIND SHELTER

Perhaps he had been conjured into the world by the mind of some tormented sleeper, perhaps he existed. There is no way of knowing. The result is that he was thrust with great force into this world by some poor woman. It is no use reflecting on what is not here and now, for everything that is not here is surely somewhere else, everything that is not here is in another place certainly but this is just too much and these things cannot will themselves to be seen by the eye. Old light which falls upon them cannot describe their forms.

As she pushed, the great force that had originated from who knows where like a wave or an animal, it's strength passed beyond what was first imagined, carried her away. She began to see colours and geometric shapes and knew by the way the peripheries of her vision darkened, closing in like a tunnel, like the end of an old cartoon, that something was very wrong.

In any case, you exist now and you're able to see the trees and the bushes.

The edges of the downy field in a jagged line cutting the powder-blue sky, thousands of flickering paper coins tied to the branches of an elegant tree. At what point did you become aware of the sculpted nature of your world? Do you imagine that this pastoral scene looked similar before the presence of man on this plane? As it is with man so it is with nature, this hidden infrastructure producing the surface phenomena we come to accept. His reality is the adornment of surfaces.

If you take a few steps inside the old church you'll see that one of the great stones of the floor is loose.

I met her in a place where people dance. She danced with her friend and I watched her for a while. I don't know how I had the courage to speak to her but I must have found it before her friend could stop her. She had been looking at me, I think she knew me although I didn't remember meeting her. I took her back to my home that night and we fucked in my home as it moved through the world. We lived together for a long while. I loved cooking for her and we spent days in and out of each other.

I MET HER IN A PLACE WHERE

The subtlety of her pussy is unparalleled. It's architecture and chemistry in perfect harmony with mine in the mist and afternoon beam of light cutting down, struck through with dust motes. If it is food and drink for a thousand years standing at the gates with just its memory it would be acceptable. If her hair was red it could also be black and acceptable. The smell of her hair is her skin following me, soft and olive with pale skin and brown hair like my sister's, like mine even!

The pink city is a memory. It had arches and was more a soft, glowing tangerine, soft, echoing architecture with no possibility of entry as if it was made of feathered cloud and flushed skin. But I did see its colonnades of rose clouds like . . .

Why has he gone? When I cry it is not really a sound, it's like friction of the mists where the crystals touch, but I know there are no crystals but only a feeling of crystals.

Like a long bell tone, soft like a bowl of breath moving out but no sound.

I started looking in earnest last week. I didn't tell anyone, I just started in the places I knew he often spends time. The coffee place is always starting early, and sometimes he has breakfast there although I told him it was a waste of money. There are a lot of people here on this pavement which goes backwards to that fellow who sings in the station. He has such a powerful voice but it always seems to me he's simulating some singing he's heard somewhere. It makes me sad and a little uncomfortable to hear it, as if he's mocking his own song.

Because I hate crowds and tight crowds in tight spaces, I never spend long in the station. The spaces between people and their smells and their perfumes I do love. If it was a woman's hair it would be different.

That was the smell of her hair, not a perfume that belonged to another woman, hot tears that came from so deep inside her accompanying sound. Like giant stones grating deep in a long moan like an animal and certainly not human sorrow.

I think I live in a ray of light, live in, moving in the ray there struck through with dust motes, his name started with eee.

Sometimes I'm in the train, here in my house in the train. I tried to go back to the place where I lost him but the morning, us, now, the afternoon. But the morning. In the smell of his bed. There is a cloud of grey perpetual, then to pink. Mist, I swim in the well of mist well. How can I be in his bed? The bed is gone. In the bed itself.

Through the crowd in the station the girl's black hair. Long boots. I'm not one of them. A black cotton top with little straps and covered in white stars.

He pushed quickly on along the green tunnel into a natural amphitheatre of trees, crossing it stage left to stage right, moving without obstruction forward, in rhythmic footfall. The old gods all present. Do not doubt this for one second, their names have not, not been forgotten either, their names are emitted directly from land. Little butterfly paper toy makes it's jittery trajectory over

golden stubs. You know why they're
here. They're coming to lift the stone.

Again, out into the open, he pushes.
There are cows and objects belonging to
men, rusting machines, small buildings
the uses of which are not known to
you. All colours green and all colours
against green. The road curves up and
away like a graceful blade. You know
what they will find there? It is not a
church, it's a temple. You know what is
under the stone. And what will you do
if you get there before them? They
have force, they know they will need it.
Beg them not lift it? Warn them? He
finds himself running along a long
colonnade of trees, without realising
how long for. He knows this place well
and he's close. Slipping on flattened
rocks hidden in the lush green grasses
he imagines breaking his leg, so close
to the temple but not close enough to
be heard calling. He imagines the
sound and the pain, the hot newness of

pain, new light, white, escaping from somewhere previously unopened. But my leg is not broken. And why do they call this place the house of god? Idiots, an empty cup! What is a cup? That was their joke, the builders. Without ever looking, you have always known it.

So it became night and I walked through the cottage. Someone had lit candles but there was no sign of this agent. Walked upstairs (although I don't recall there being an upstairs?) and through to the right, into the last room, the one on the corner with the two doors. I played with my shadow on the chalky, uneven wall. I held up an empty birdcage in such a way that it seemed my arm was the branch of a tree from which it was hanging.

I was admiring the effect when I saw a second shadow, though there was no one else in the room as far as I could discern. Thinking it my own, I looked closer. I recoiled when I saw that it was not a shadow but a darkened, living projection in which I could make out your features. You had lost weight and your hair was in a boyish cut but it was clearly you.

I ran from that place in tears and kept running until I was flying. I went for so long that I lost consciousness.

When he awoke he was with the group of pilgrims again. They had been sleeping in a little natural dish near the edge of the cliff, covered with a single tarpaulin. There were a couple of rocks embedded in the earth of the crater but it made a convenient protection. It had obviously been used for this purpose in the past by other travelers. The guides had started preparing the vulgar, black, salty tea that he had now become used to. How was it? That this foul beverage had taken its place in him? He knew that he had not only accepted it but would miss it if he returned alive. They began walking early.

His joints took a while to warm. His calf and thigh muscles, still tight from the previous day's walking, gave little twinges as he walked the narrow and uneven grey path.

As they turned an outcropping of rocks they beheld the source of the sound. Sat on the highest of four peaks like the peaks of a crown was a man and from him emanated this sound, this sound of an opening tunnel, the sound of a gate held open. It was a held note whose harmonics twisted and what emanated from him could be seen by the mind's view as neither foam nor sound, neither smoke nor sparks but all of them and projected from his seated body to the cardinal points of the earth. Perhaps it was not a man, they barely asked themselves. Yet they all saw it as real for they were so tired and changed from their procession round the great mountain. Perhaps it was a woman.

And everyday he would get dressed a little early, take a couple of steps to the kitchen and reach for the bags that were kept on the fridge. At the first sound of crinkling crackling plastic, her little dog would begin such an excited whooping and jumping that it was a relief when he put the little loop of the strange bridle lead around her muzzle. The first time he had taken her out he could not understand how the configuration of metal rings and straps fit round both the neck and mouth of the little dog.

After ten minutes of unbearable yapping he settled just for the strap around her neck. He regretted this choice almost instantly on stumbling into the daylight. The tiny grey being had yanked and yapped it's way around the peopled streets, strangling itself with every step.

We walked many times but we never,
as I recall, saw him.

After a while they fell into a little routine
that comforted them both. After closing
the street door behind them it would
be only a few metres before she
flattened her rear to the cobbles of the
rue de Lappe and pissed a good puddle
that ran down between the convex
stones to the gutter. Grateful that after
a few more steps there was the little
alley into which they could turn. Their
ritual was well established and at the
end of this first alley she would shit the
first of two stools, for which he would
be ready with the first of the bags. He
had no interest in dwelling on her shit
but couldn't help feeling like a Roman
physician observing the Emperor's health
by scrutiny of the Royal productions.

She was an unbearably sweet little
creature who was only afraid of people
skating, having been traumatized by

some vile rider in her past who kicked her so hard she had never forgotten it. As they walked she would turn her head back regularly to check her chaperone was well, especially at crossings and junctures. The sound of her feet on the stones was the sound of a delicate wind-up toy or a stopwatch perfectly rhythmic and regular, tick tick ticking out her animal joy.

The walks had taken a regular route, starting with the alley, looping round two blocks and back through that alley to form the outline of a balloon on a string or a comic book speech bubble. The speech bubble always contained the same text: "I love you, I really need to shit, I love you . . ." That dog never existed. If she did she would be 38 years old now. I miss you so much. I also looked in the transporter. I looked whenever there was a Wednesday.

The seats in the transporter looked old, hard-molded and the blue colour of a grandmother's bath tub. They had no place in that century.

It was peopled with a selection of tired and depressed workers, dreading whatever they had to do that day to fight off destitution. A fat man in tired jeans and a pink shirt open too low dipped in and out of sleep. His lower lip jutted in his somnolence and his strange, medieval, yellowing hair rose revealing a hairy neck. In his half sleep he clutched a free newspaper containing the type of non information one can expect when one pays nothing. If you pay nothing then you have bought nothing. On the front page a picture of an idyllic lakeside with hammocks and a shady picnic, the words HOW DOES LUXURY CAMPING TEMPT YOU? in large letters. Yet it was quite clear that for him there would be no electric and no luxury camping. The best he could hope for was an edible dinner this evening. No important or successful people ever rode the transporter. Other similar magazines had images even more absurd: gold bars. Gold bars? Who would believe that to be a credible outcome? Their hopes had been reduced to the fantasies of children. Because they had their filters set quite high, we could only read some of their superficial thoughts. Most of them were thinking about sleeping on the . . . fucking . . . phone . . . wishing they had been to the toilet before they left the station.

As the craft began the turn before its descent towards the tunnel it hit an air pocket and one of the gyroscopic coaches made a strange hook upwards, jolting the occupants and throwing them against each other and that is how a woman with a bad corkscrew perm spilled hot coffee on her skirt . . .

AT ANY MOMENT

His neck is a tube—
his head is a box—
he is the smartest of all the robots!

It seems this shopping centre is my
home now, although it wasn't designed
as a home. It existed, I'm quite certain,
between days. It is now Thursday
although, because of the weather and
the new spring light, the longer days, it
seems like a Friday.

All of the shops here sell absolutely nothing of use unless you are one of the girls that stand outside the clubs. Are they prostitutes? If they are, their business is so discreet as to be imperceptible. All of the food they sell here is for them. It is not the food of their native countries—no one knows what that would look like—but it's food that they understand nevertheless. They sell weapons also, extendable blackjacks, neural disrupters, crossbolt throwers, strange grenades filled with tiny yellow gas pellets. Who buys them? I'm here every day and I've never seen anyone buy anything in any of the boutiques other than ugly sports shoes. I do see men staring at these objects in the display, with a distant look in their eyes and I know exactly what they are thinking. Many times I have wished I'd had one of these instruments in my hand at a given moment, when the most satisfactory action would be to pin the face of some piece of human excrement to the wall with a bolt of

certainty. They are thinking of an equal-
izing power. They are thinking of laughter
and the fragility of human tissue.

"They're just notes, just the air vibrating.
Why should it have this effect on me? I
don't get it . . . they're just sounds!" The
foreigner stared out at the road. After a
few seconds he turned his head back
towards the park and his interlocutor.

"You know damn well there's no such
thing as 'just notes', he said. Unless
everything else has this status . . . they
are just the mathematically beautiful
patterns of leaves, this is just the best
roast chicken sandwich I've ever eaten,
She is just the love of your life."

"But why did I tell them of my plans?"
Said the foreigner.

Everybody knows there is no surer way
of crushing a plan in the womb than to
tell people about it.

It's because I am an amiable soul. It's because I'm happy to tell people of my passions that my plans almost always come to nothing. Yes, there it is. There's always an explanation. That must be it."

"You want to live but you are afraid. The girl in the bakery is beautiful, you imagine yourself between her legs. The girl in the second office is beautiful and you imagine yourself locked inside her like two pieces of a puzzle. But you won't do it. You want to wake up in cotton sheets in New York, in Rio with a god who smells of spice in leather. You want to stand on the steppes and plains of forgotten worlds but it will never be.

Your mind is writing cheques that your life cannot cash.

This is the shadow and this is the way it casts, the tension is the coffee you drink to survive and as I look at the cup," said the interlocutor, who by now was standing to leave. "I realize it wasn't me who drank it."

We are back in the transporter with its blues and polished steel.

"Now do you understand why?" he said, "they are just worms. Look at them. They're distinguished only by the addition of limbs, which, when seen in the light of reason appear to be superfluous, artifice. What could raise them above this status? What could render them more noble? I dare you, I defy you to give me proofs that it can be done. Just because you have dreams of flight, over moonlit fields, over silver farmlands under electricity lines and up into billowing clouds, and to the edges of sleeping cities, this does not mean that in daylight you are not a worm. You are that, and in that you can have faith, but only in that. Proofs in the scientific sense of the term. What signs do you see that you could aspire to a more noble station? This is not the voice of an angry parent, this is not the penultimate link denying the last and final circle, what he was denied in turn. You never lacked love or means. you were deprived only of a noble soul and by no visible agency either. You are not even facing it, that you might one day arrive, at your crawling pace. Mahdi does not come, and you are not lacking in strength or beauty but, worse yet, you are uninteresting. The worst of crimes and one that you started committing at birth. You were not locked under a staircase. You were not beaten, you were not punished unduly. Your retouched memories are of tents in warm gardens, of cats and pianos. If you went to dig in dirt it was your play, your choice. Don't you know? You can only want what you want. You can never want what you want to want.

You are like a little dog on the beach barking at the waves!"

From this vantage point it would seem
that their reason for being is to destroy
the fabric of their universe. They would
have you believe you'd arrived at the end,
that the seas were acid. It seems you
arrived when the world was coughing,
slightly. It still seemed strong and all
powerful. Now it is certainly dying. I
defy you to prove otherwise.

And yet they cannot. As tenacious as
they are, it is they who will be destroyed.
They will undo their world. And if all
the rarest beings are lost, new ones will
arise more splendid than those departed.
Why is this? Because the world is outside our time. It does not need our pity.
Why is it that I can see this and all these
things and yet I cannot find him?

Ox lows
Horn sounds
A gate is open
This is your chance
Go now

I can't seem to eat these days. I would like to, the food looks so appetizing but I can't, I no longer have the requisite tools. Since it's every day (there are not really days as such), it's hard to adapt. I can eat the smells that fall through. Just be careful that you don't arouse Cutmond's interest. The last thing we need is that animal intervening.

It's finally happening happnn-nn-nuh—space unfolds constantly in such a way that decried . . . Oh, Mr Simpson's here or whatever his name was, the one with the RADA voice who sat with you on the cusp of the hill. You remember, near box hill. He was dressed strangely that day. I mean he was wearing its tiny body. He was 'it' at that moment I suppose.

Ok, well, then you start. Start from the beginning.

They sat on the cusp of the little ridge looking out across the South Downs. It was a warm afternoon with a grassy chlorophyll smell rising in the drying sun. Below them, a patchwork of irregular fields cut by hedgerows and stiles at odd angles. Bracken and grasses and oaks and beeches and horse chestnuts extending into the distance. Blue with a few white tufts slowly forming. Marc looked down at Mr Simpson and then to his side, to the right, the Arch Demon Bathael.

"It's difficult I know," said Mr Simpson, "But please try to bear with me, dear boy. There is no way to explain this type of thing so you will just have to make do." He could feel his tiny hands on his leg through his jeans as he patted around. "Do you recognize this?"

"Yes," said Marc

"I've chosen this form because I thought it would make this easier for you, simpler. I'm sorry if it's a little incongruous.

This is the impenetrable, you will never see the source, only the reflected light, do you see?"

Marc said nothing. He gazed at Mr Simpson's little eyes like taught, black fish eggs, his nose, his whiskers. This plummy voice of love and authority emanated from what seemed to be a shuddering field mouse.

He turned to the hulking demon to his right. A hot sound like rainbow-oil vapour escaped his jaw from the crab-like folds and spines of his mouth which was like an emitting oven. Long hissing sounds. His oily skin was not skin with his oily scales of hardened dried blood. He glistened. The grass around him sizzled. He sat three times higher than a man, the air his blistering and puffing aura. Bat-like and insect-like, his onyx bones penetrated and left his flesh at impossible angles. He was hard and he shone black, squatting and looking out at the same scene the others saw with an expression of animal hate and confusion.

A chaffinch flew by, tracing a curve against the blue.

"Haaaaakkkhhhhgggggrrrrrraaaaaahhh hkkk-khhhh," said the demon, his head swiveling like a mounted gun on a giant oiled bearing to follow it across the near sky.

Marc was not able to speak.

"Yes," Said Mr Simpson," I understand that you are frightened, dear fellow. It is quite natural that you are very frightened but I assure you that he can do you no harm here. He holds no power in this place." He patterfooted into Marc's open hand and put his tiny hands onto his wrist.

Marc's heart was beating at an extremely fast pace.

"Yes, yes. Perhaps this was a clumsy gesture but I brought him here to illustrate a point, so please don't be afraid.

There was never a time, only stolen honey, do you see? They all still love you as you love them. As you ever loved them. Even before there was a you there ever was. It can not be said, neither here nor on any stone that dances around any fire that makes up the milk of the heavens. Its shadow is seen everywhere. It's source nowhere etc. I was never very good at this sort of thing so forgive me if . . ."

"Behold, I am Bathael bbaelalkhhhav, Extinguisher of Eyes and Souls, Hider of Keyes," the demon straightened, in a measured sound, between purring and the grinding of stone blocks, "Dual

Feeder of All Sufferings. Engenderer of Torments." As if speaking phrases he had learned in a language not his own, "Subdivider of Bodies, I who am anointed, who sits by the side of the Great Desecrator . . ."

"Oh, do shut up," said Mr Simpson, "you are tiresome."

The demon was utterly silent and gazed ever more confusedly into the farthest distance. An expression approaching childish uncertainty could be read among the obsidian features of his terrifying countenance.

"He has no idea where he is, none whatsoever. He has never before left the realm where he was imagined. He can exercise none of his energies here, Which is a good thing because he can do such terrible things."

Mr Simpson feeling Marc's heart slowing slightly, scurried back to his knee, his pinkish-brown tail hanging off to one side. He turned and looked up at Marc.

"But in the end it is for him that I feel the most sorrow. Let sorrows and sins be collars and pins. He is the one that must inhabit that foulness and who knows where he earned that honour."

As if hearing a long forgotten rhyme, the giant demon chimed in: "it is my honour to serve the Great Desecrator, vile diminisher of . . ."

"No," said Mr Simpson softly, "you are a guest here and you will say nothing more." *Avanh guratpalan niav*, remember, you we're not summoned here by some local lackey," he said, almost laughing.

"You see," he said addressing Marc again, "he is no more real than any of this. Although he has swept across lands and waters befouling and embittering all within. Not even real, you see?"

"Do you know where he is?" said Marc finally, "do you think he will come?"

"Do you remember the story of the sea turtle and the floating hoop? I used to tell it to you when you were very young. You loved that story but you were afraid of it. Maybe he is already there?"

"By the way, I hate to be the one to tell you this. You're not actually Marc. There was never a real Marc."

What would a survival plan look like at this point?

I have the option at all times. If I look to the left of whatever I'm looking at, it's there, the too bright gate thing sometimes changing. There it is! Like a small black electronic croak. Croaking. Why are you murmuring? If you have something to say just say it.

Ok, said the sound, If there is something to succeed then I have failed because no one will ever love me like you did. No one will love me like the little dog does. No one will.

And with this he turned and threw his jeweled spear into the sun.

I will always love you. Even when love is no more. When there is nothing.

The spear passed the manifold golden lips of the sun-mouth of the sun, through day and turned it into night, into the throat of the sun through thought, into dream and wish. And likeness. You are not, you are a likeness.

"This seems a good place to cross. Let's cross here."

"The lake is too deep, I can't even see the bottom, I'm not sure about this."

"You can swim, what are you worried about? Do you really want to go around again? We're always going around."

"No, I don't want to go around again . . . is it dangerous?"

"I don't know."

"Well, are there animals in there?"

"Yes, there can be."

"Then of course it's fucking dangerous."

As the sound of the transporter dies down you can hear the voices of the occupants softly rising up to fill the space it left.

I have looked in many places, even a toilet cubicle.

The coat hook in the toilet cubicle is a sign of civilization. In this case the coat hook looks like an octopus netsuke and, bearing this in mind, I must tell you that . . .

Last night I went through a different passage whose aperture was as tiny as the eye of a needle, like passing through the orbits of an electron. But somehow I managed to go through, and you would be surprised just how far away that place was. I tried looking in that place where I was still married to my old wife. Her face . . . she looked so happy and so sorrowful.

"Where were you?" she said, "You've been away for years."

I tried to stay there but it was very far away in the night sky through space.

I did manage to live there for while but eventually I would start to meet people who cried and said I was their husband also. They had the same look on their faces. Disbelief, joy and horror. I had to try and send messages back through the tunnel. I tried to get other people to call you and explain where I was.

The phone calls were very distant white noise as they too had to pass through the tiny aperture

"Wasn't there a flood at your school where the bus started sinking into the playing field?" said the little white noise at the end of the line.

"Yes, but that was years ago. I was in the driver's seat of that bus which was sticking out of a field, by that time very dry and overgrown with summer grasses."

When I returned the little dog was so excited. She didn't care that I was different and jumped up and down with the same joy when she saw me. In the end I could feel this world collapsing and would have to say goodbye and lie down, lie down as the whole thing spun and collapsed in. The last thing I did was fight gravity to lift my hand and wave little goodbyes. Through old light.

Old light, old fire arriving, puncturing and punctuating the heavens.

ALL PERMUTATIONS WILL EVENTUALLY BE EXPENDED UNTIL

Eventually even the plastic bee on the spring and his two strange animal companions, who stood like a coven in the little children's play area, they too became gods. They received offerings, songs of devotion and the veneration of all animals high and low. They granted visions to lowly emissaries and princes. they sent prophets and messengers and saviors who brought their light and wisdom into the world. At one point I was even considered as a candidate to be one of them but, as you know, I refused. And their adversaries also became known. Bathael, Cutmond. In this place a day was 2 hours and 17 minutes longer and the night was equally augmented. This meant people (if one can call them people, for they were evolved from objects) had more time to rest and do their daily activities. Whatever activities these plastic beings have on a daily basis. Of course it also left more time for searching.

I must have drifted off for a moment while searching and when I opened my eyes again the festival had come to life. After all the noisy preparations and the arrival of the Great Agni, filling the air with her new light. In this festival the air filled with invisible particles which destroy tissue and mutate bones. The city is much the same as ever except more soot and ash and the old woman is being eaten alive in broad daylight in the boulevard because she was too slow.

She had been rifling through a plastic bin with a folded in, toothless face. I feel like I am her face sometimes, folding inwards. It seems rather a violent festival, what with all the vomiting of blood and burns and urinating of blood and rectal bleeding with no supper and no support to the human frame and the soot. I hope it doesn't happen often. That would be terrible.

At least I'm reassured by the chain that hangs from my hand every day unless it's the other weapon. I want to assure you, that chain was never chosen as a weapon although I suppose it had crossed my mind that if anyone tried to harm the little dog I know it would quickly become one. Otherwise it is the straight razor that becomes the weapon. It is at once a divine and guilty object into which is enfolded the potential for separating, dividing and subdividing, draining and leeching, tapping, changing lives forever. I carry it sometimes and its presence changes me. I have seen men, angry men, recoil without seeing it as if they sensed the presence of the object. I have only ever used it as a warning, only left small marks. I couldn't bring myself to let it unfold as it pleases. Only Cutmond would be capable of that.

I wait for long periods at a time. It is my strength and also a type of weakness, this capacity to wait. Something that I must have learned in the prison. In that little room. One would hear voices in that room where only two others came, and waiting was defiance. The little dog told me that she knows how to transform the time into physical objects. If I watch her long enough she is like any other human.

When I first entered the prison I had gone there to help someone else but they called my name in the waiting room and I was forced to stay. It took a long while to believe it was real. The sliding doors, the receptionist, the waiting room. The weird, two-piece combination suit in blue. It was half empty and only sometimes would we see the driver and his wife bring people to and from the green metal gates.

They speak none of the languages I was taught. Sweets, candies. They (my kind visitors) brought me too many, once, and I made myself sick but it was so nice.

All writing is prison writing. All real thought is monastic thought.

Light comes aching forth as if from a gulley lined with hanging trees. Greened yellow light, like the morning of a prophet's arrival, a dream dawn like any other. Banal day, perfect.

Doom time.

Hell time.

Tunnel transportation.

This is cutting at the root of my dream. I wish to kill the dream.

As the pilgrims entered the first chamber I realized that my bones still echoed the recent pain. It is wet under foot and apart from the preparation of the surfaces which is part of the ritual and we are allowed to sing as we are alone. Sometimes I'm tired of the wet and dirty work and imagine myself one of the dignitaries who will finally use this place. They must never think of our sweat and our trials but we are preparing the chambers with colour. Building the towers is a long and protracted task. Generations pass in the time it takes us to prepare the first edifice. With what I have learned I can make the surfaces of the tunnels into green leather or ice or aged copper or dusty chalky powdered like the walls in that far house, that little house on the island, in the mountain. Or like gold or the ochre walls of a medieval doge's palace.

Before I met the elders, I once made the wall of one tiny chamber into an anemone of translucent blue arms. I passed my hand through them. I had never crafted anything of that delicacy. They waved and softly brushed at nothing as if swayed by an invisible current. In moonlight. Although there could not have been moonlight in such tunnels.

In cold mornings the air is milky pale with wet dust hanging. In the tunnels that run beneath and through the edifice for long swathes of time, all the places are connected by these tunnels . . . I spent days walking in these tunnels knowing full well I would not find anything here. Nothing can live here, there is no light, new or old. Whatever light you need must be carried in vessels and woe to you if you haven't enough. You are held, enclosed in the field of light you carry. Once the light goes so do you, stretched out in all directions, pulled into the corridors, to fill with yourself, these tunnels with no end. Stretched atom-thin on the rack of dark space. I walked and sang sometimes stooping. Droning songs that fit very well into the chambers.

At parties or places where people dance, Cutmond often appears. Cutmond is a rare devil. A rare fucking devil indeed. He raises his glass to his lips, a glass full of fire that he tests on others.

He looks confident enough but I know two things: he loves the spontaneous, bewildered weakness caused by a show of force or guile or an unannounced spectacle of terror. And that he hates himself and, therefore, all women.

When I first met him he was a lovable boy with bright eyes. It's hard now to imagine his kiddish laugh, knowing the harm he has done. But he has suffered most by all accounts.

I AM THE PET IN THE MOUNTAIN DESERT

As I search it becomes clear that there has been a mistake. It was frustrating at first. The eye is drawn to imperfections. Either to beautiful objects or hideous objects. Now I seem to see all objects, except of course, the one I'm searching for. No single object has importance over another. Sometimes I can see through them. To be those objects. It is as if a vial has been shattered and a gas has escaped, hissing into everything.

It is very much like the pink gas we saw from the transporter when we were children. They said it was just the colour of the dawn through thick fog but we knew they had finally done it. They had released the gas. Do you not see the corresponding time line? That must be when it started.

He walks up the concrete stairs to the blue door on the second floor. It strikes him as strange that this should be the place where there is an entrance to the tunnels. They trust each other and have

been pilgrims together. The other three
are in a similar condition, laughing
exhausted. They have been searching
together for 48 hours without rest and
this is a holy day.

One of them has the key.

They have barely entered the blood-
coloured corridor to the chamber when
the northerner is producing the package.
Instead of following the ceremonial steps
he divides the contents between them
equally.

"That looks too much."

"There is no such thing."

No sooner has he said this, than he is
trying to consume his whole share in
one. It is clear that it is too much as he
cannot keep it all in his mouth. Yet, still
they do it, all three of them.

He felt instantly hoisted into the air with an accompanying rising frequency in his ears and teeth until, as if spat out of a mouth, he found himself outside himself. His body slid to the floor.

Unlike the normal hallucinations and babbling that are associated with the ritual, there was only one prophetic phrase spoken before all of them were crawling, invisible to each other. He was like a pet who was writhing and . . . when I was a boy, very near to here, there was fight, with the taste of blood and far from home.

Here, eyes close. "I am outside for the first time."

Here, the music is the life eternal pounding like waves, hammering a hole in this dimension. The time extends away in all directions through the newly created gate. The gate is on every side.

"There is time but I am now outside it. Of course! The body is the event in time. Like a slow-motion firework of meat and bone which explodes at birth and dims at death."

The waves of music are deep and bright.

"I'm not alone here. Who could be here if I am not here? I have no self, how can there be anyone else here, outside?"

A warm voiceless voice: "Why are you here?"

"I think I'm searching"

Warm voiceless voice: "Why don't you start by returning and being kind to others?"

Imperceptibly.

The other two are crawling and vomiting, their bodies rejecting the substance.

I search on various islands. The first one is covered in vines and figs and birds and little troupes of monkeys walking along the tarmac in the early morning. There is a little house there with white chalky walls (although they have at one time been made of bamboo and some woven reeds) and it is the one where your shadow was projected on the wall, but in the mountains. The island is hot and there are fireflies at night around the tops of the trees and telephone poles. The sand is always either pure white or it is black volcanic sand that keeps the heat. One exception: when we walked along that sand in the moonlight so clear it was like a woodcut but powdery. Because of the phosphorescent plankton washed up in the sand that night, our footprints lit up electric blue. Miracle phenomena. Sometimes it is just black volcanic rock cut into a ledge from which children are diving. This is the island where I heard him speaking very softly and I could almost forget that she was searching.

The second island had long palm trees literally falling into crystal waters, their roots showing in giant semicircles rising from the sand. I searched at the village, in the diorama at the end of that covered place where people dance with the low walls. In it is a scene with a tiger standing over a prone man pulling at his intestines through an open hole in his stomach. The goddess stands to his left on a pile of skulls, eyes wide, her tongue extended. She has many arms holding different objects of power, including the folded chain and the straight razor. At the right are two children and a little dog. All the players in this scene are painted and lacquered with what appears to be clear honey.

They do not move, although if you focus on one of them for long enough, you will see movement at the corner of your eye. This is because you are creating a tunnel outside of which they are real but you are not. He found nothing in there except nauseating meat, but the children sitting on that low wall stared at him and at the scene and laughed. There is too much heat, my shirt is wet and there are contours of white salt on the back. The air is thick. So he decided to return at night to the wooden cottage.

IN WOMEN

They met in a place where people dance. In the Droom. She saw him dancing and to be honest, at first he was probably looking at another girl behind her (and let's face it that is what they were, girls in their 20s, for good or bad, not yet women). Somehow she was a beacon and he saw through her a beautiful radiance. He saw, yes, warm surface. And yet he saw through her as if through a gate into a night-like darkness in which there was a second light. The beacon. They danced and bumped their bodies shedding shadows like reptile skins onto the floor around each other and then talked, and he found her simple in her intentions. She was ready to take the step off the high platform, make a jump into her own night-like darkness.

In him she saw an absence of the horrors and dangers of the complicated heart. He was strange and funny. This is a moment of alignment of time proceeding, where the gate opens its fiery mouth aperture, if just for an hour, showing ink-blue corridors rarely seen. The starry inner organs.

I write her a letter which is also a poem and it comes from a place of symbols. It speaks of a harvest, of a silver thread that extends into deep space, the origin of which is in the heart. Even I do not know its true meaning so if you have read it and can make some sense of it, please do because I find it troubling.

But, in any case, she read it and must have been touched by it because on their next meeting they all but ran to her bed pulling at each other's clothes. It was as if something else had usurped the communication.

They walked together in the little park by his house at dusk until they came to the lake. It was of a considerable size for a suburban area and, it being dusk, the air was filled with bats patrolling the sky and swooping over the mirror of water. He had prepared some little pieces of food in a bag which he produced from his pocket. The light from the nearby lamps was a yellow-orange and, to some degree, bleached out the benches and trees.

"What's that?"

"Bat food"

"What do you mean?"

"I mean food for the bats"

"What? No way. You can't feed wild bats."

"Can and have!"

"'Haha! What do you feed them?"

"Little bits of ham and bread."

"That's ridiculous, they eat insects."

"They . . . I don't know if they eat it, but look!"

He began taking the little pieces and throwing them into the air above the water. As he did this, the bats would swoop in tight circles and catch the tiny pieces of meat and bread in mid air. They were fascinated at this supernatural feat and paused between each offering to appreciate the scene. The water was still as glass and, despite the polluting light from the street lamps, the stars were visible in the water, giving the illusion that the sky and the water were one. It was as if they were standing at the edge of the world and looking into space.

At one moment, ripples expanded from a point quite close to them in the water, warping the surface which contained the lower space and stars. It could have been that a bat had touched the mirror with its wing or, more likely, that a piece of food had escaped, falling into the pool. In any case, as soon as this happened, the bats, no longer trusting their mirror, retreated temporarily to a higher plane. He wiped off his hand and kissed her in the cool air. It seemed to last for a thousand years. If it were food and drink for a thousand years it would be acceptable. When it ended, he held her left hand in his right and looked back at the stars in the settled water.

The light had changed and something could now be seen in the water. At first they assumed it must be a reflection but after a few seconds, bemused and wide-eyed, it dawned on them that no such thing could be possible. There, in the water, was a sleeping giant, painted a blueish-green. He seemed to be lying on what looked like a bed of giant black tubes or eels or car tires. As the water calmed it was clear that his hands were in strange, fixed postures and that he was surrounded by luminous spheres or bubbles like marbles with swirls of light and matter inside them. In his hair were three broaches representing a bull, a dog and a snake. He appeared to be floating in space because of this illusion. The giant was clearly alive and sleeping. In his sleep his lips moved and seemed to be repeating a phrase. Their instinct was to try and decode the phrase but as soon as they began, a leaf or a piece of something fell into the waters of space disturbing the lower sky once more. The apparition lasted seconds but felt like an eternity. The celestial reflections were there, but the giant was gone. Everything is loss. At all times this is true. Passing. This is the horror and the beauty.

"How did you become someone else? It's no longer you."

"Make no mistake. It is me."

I will now take a little time to describe to you some of the contents of the Droom.

In the Droom there is a strange automaton made of wood and brown metal. He appears to be a type of copper and has the overall colour of old pennies. He is incredibly detailed and the strata of his joints, which are held in place by tiny studs allow him a remarkable range of expression with only very slight movement. His eyes have beveled brass rims and beautiful polished lenses of convex glass, and his mouth is a compact network of articulated sections forming a contoured plane. He sits like a zoetrope attraction in the corner of an old amusement arcade. Opposite him is a dressmaker's dummy. It is a female form covered in a cream-coloured canvas with no real features.

Often, at a particular time in the afternoon, possibly after school, there is a young boy who enters and puts a coin into a slot in the machine's neck.

At this point, as you may have guessed from memory, there is a little whirring, fluttering sound and two bright cones of light spring from those very eye sockets. They have darker beams moving within them. They are flecked through with swirling dust motes. They superimpose, if you follow them, to focus on the now beautiful mannequin and she gestures. She is very lovely, and though she makes no sound we can read her lips. The apertures widen and the little layers of copper around his mouth shift to form a little smile. She says the same thing in various different ways. Sometimes it is a different face or you may have changed your hair to a more boyish cut but it is always you. The only sound is the crackle of a distant song that has eroded with a thousand plays. I cannot remember the name of that song but at the end of this worn recording we can just make out a few seconds of the barking of the little dog as the last chords fade.

I must stress that the Droom is neither place nor a specific place, as such, but *various places* which can be reached by corridor (or tunnel), with the whole thing remaining, to a certain extent, corridor.

By the way, did I mention that I was ripped apart back there? The substance must have been stronger than I thought because what began with the appearance of little wheels of squatting men holding hands like Aztec decorations, emerging from and, projected onto every surface like interlocking gears, like looking into its gears. There is a breach in the air . . . it is rent and ripped—ripped open. Ripped and flapping like a curtain in the wind as time rushes through the open wound.

It was then that I realized that the sword I had been sharpening was the sword of my own execution. I paused for a while in deep reflection. Finally I began working again with even greater vigour, for who could have a greater stake in the blade's efficacy than the condemned man.

"Are you sure that he exists? From what I can tell, there seems to be little evidence. What are you basing this assumption on?"

"I know he exists. The Prime Guardian confirmed it with her gestures many times. She has saved many from terrifying ends and, occasionally, I have saved her. It's true, her actions seem perverse. She sometimes consumes garments which contain the vital traces of those she protects. She has been known to act in unconventional ways but she is the only one I can trust. Her heart is undivided. Her heart is certain, for it has only one objective—the primary objective. When one opens the sealed casks of funerary remains from the First Kingdom, her clay likeness is often to be found wrapped in a cloth containing seeds and honey, placed on the breast of the deceased.

The bronze from which her statues are made was forged at the first civil union. She was worshipped with misguided ritual in the Indus Valley and the Tigris-Euphrates delta for many millennia, although, recently, she has taken this innocuous form in order to spend more time with specific cases. Can you imagine blood spilt for her, she who placed the jewels at the junctures of the web? That task was undertaken with such patience. I've seen her waiting in silence for aeons only to come to life as soon as there was love to be given.

I don't know why it took me so long to recognize her. Perhaps it is because her hair was cut differently."

It is a shining day at the end of the world outside. Time is a long note of light from the reverb of three notes on a frozen

piano glancing off the buildings. Shining
cubes and lozenges, like the wings of
aircraft, the air molecules around them
sizzling in the cold air. A black priest
in his robes, the ladies in their prints.
Lumpen men with moist lower lips.

It is, of course, another day now and
I'm no closer to knowing where he has
passed.

It is sometimes hard to remember where
in the transporter—there—falling like
the friction of light from distant stars, to
put my finger on it or mist as a man he
was so handsome and had the body of a
19-year-old through time. Have you seen
him? I'm starting to fear for his safety.

Lest there should be any confusion at this
point about his previous whereabouts
before the Droom, I should just clarify.

After careful examination, I can surmise
that the entrance to the Droom and all

adjoining tunnels is like that of a wicker fish trap. That is to say that it is very easy to slip into but almost impossible to exit, as the opening is like a flap that falls back, becoming flush with the walls. I spent such a long time running my fingers along the surface trying to find the seam where flap touched wall. Now I feel that even had I found it, I would have needed an instrument so fine to slide between the two pieces that it would have been invisible at one end.

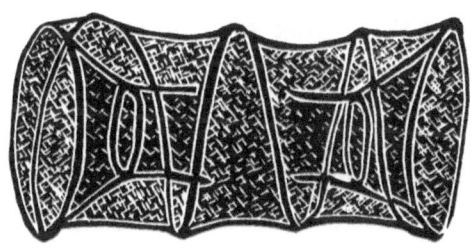

Some people have mistakenly imagined that there was an exit to the Droom *inside* people and many have been needlessly killed in this way. Cut open, disemboweled, their intestines and organs rummaged through in the hope of finding some way out. Whole towns were put to the sword in this way. Men women and children gutted like fish on the off chance that an exit could be found. Instead of their hearts desire, all that was produced was tons of stinking offal, flies and floods of crimson blood, smelling of iron and excrement, until they were ankle-deep in it. Those who were eviscerated were in some ways luckier than those who did the killing, for at least they didn't have to try to understand it.

This was originally a perversion of a simpler idea and is believed to have been based on a rumour instigated by Cutmond many thousands of years ago.

No, I think I have chosen wisely to continue my search within the Droom itself.

One of the tunnels has a mouth in New Mexico. It opens from the ground and one climbs out of it as if appearing from a manhole. From the outside, the opening is a rectangle of tarmac on a wide truck stop parking space, although to the touch it feels like a flap of leather.

Again, the flap, once dropped, re-seals itself, like a perfectly healed wound, leaving no sign of its existence. I suppose I could have jammed it open with my shoe but, as always, these things happen so quickly. No, I decided to stay and watch the vast electrical storm which unfurled all around. I have seen this one before (in fact it is almost always the same storm, with its smell of wet dust and negative ions) but it never loses its appeal. They warn against standing out in storms of this type. The vast volumes of water and electricity have an undesirable effect when introduced to bodies, but I have always stayed out in it. If I head towards the light and shelter of the store there will only be products. Sugar, oil, root beer, cinnamon gums, dried beef, chocolate bars. There is no use looking there. Believe me, I have already tested that path. I have spent an inordinate amount of time circumambulating those isles, again and again. He never eats those types of things, he considers them poisons. So he won't be there. I will continue looking in the morning when my head is rested.

During my dream that night, I flew over that same tarmac, seeing the buses and trucks arranged in their diagonal spaces. From above, the light spilled out from the truck stop in a diffused L-shape from the two walls which have windows. I accelerated up through the storm clouds until I was above them looking down

on the clouds lit by that same powdery,
cartoon moon.

> Oh demon star
> Oh fragrant star
> Oh perfumed light
> Oh host of all nights
> Oh guardian
> Oh sentinel
> That guards himself
> I beseech thee
> I implore thee
> With tribute high
> Consuming fire
> Consuming flesh
> Grant me passage
> To the farthest side

"Really? That's what you said? That's
how you asked? I'm sorry but that really
is rubbish. No wonder you can't find
him."

The city had all but cleared. It was a
pleasure to walk. The rich and the

fortunate had scattered to the corners of the globe to notch up another geographical anecdote to brandish at the first soirée of their return. Those who remained were the poorest and most troubled. As it was, Paris was a magnet for the bitter and deranged. The mentally derailed staring about, talking to themselves, muttering. The city now had the strange atmosphere of an insane museum, a tourist asylum.

My watch says its 5:20 but it could be wrong. My heart says it's 5:17 but that's because it has stopped and always tells the same time. If it began ticking again there would be a fucking rumble in the jungle.

I am looking at the girl's black cotton top on the transporter. It is covered in stars. I'm . . . falling into space

1ST ASCENT

As I recall, they were both 13 or 14 years old, between children and adults, yet neither. They were rash and decided that on the day of fasting it would be appropriate to start making their way down the cliffs to the plateau below. They were not even dressed for any kind of climbing or tracking but simply began with the blind reasoning that all would go well for them.

They were such good friends, they had shared things that others probably would not have shared. They shared unconditional love and would have certainly given their lives for each other at any moment if it had been necessary. They had spent many nights breaking into various official buildings, houses and even museums. They both knew that the punishment for this would have been terrible had they been caught, but, somehow, by some miracle, it never happened.

They would break into the houses of people they knew and go through their belongings, not to steal anything but simply because they could. It gave them power in their powerless world. They could climb well, they could enter small windows and tight spaces. They had learned to use each other as ladders and pull one another up when walls seemed unassailable. It was part of their love. They would light fires on the tiled floors of the houses they entered, which they controlled. The fires would grow only to the size they chose. They were discovering their penises and would feel nothing strange about playing with them in the presence of their other half, their partner. They were not excited by each other. They were excited by women or the images of women they had found. By the underwear of women they knew to live in the houses. They had ultimate power in these places, so it's no wonder that they felt invincible that afternoon on that fasting day.

Of course they didn't take the road. They did not want the road. They wanted to go straight down and they believed they could reach the bottom because they had seen it clearly. It had not occurred to them that there are many things one can see but not reach. Who is to tell a young god what he can do?

As they climbed down they talked and laughed and spoke of each other's friends and cousins who they had never seen but imagined they would love to fuck. They talked about traveling and cars, the cars they would have when they drove away from this place. It was a beautiful place with clouds coming towards you as you stood on the cliff edge, that enveloped you in fog on their arrival. They dreamed of sex and fucking with beautiful, exotic women, and food for it was a fasting day. Their stupidly inappropriate shoes slipped on the gravel and rocks as they skated and climbed and made their way arrogantly down.

"What about that cousin? She's so beautiful, you think she would want to do it with me?"

"Which one?"

"I don't know her name, she's your cousin, the one in the photo with the beautiful, almond-shaped eyes."

"Oh my god! She's not even my cousin and you can't fuck her, I can't even fuck her and if anyone is going to fuck her, it's me."

"So what's her name? What's her name?"

"I think it's Asia, something like that, it's some kind of weird name."
"Yeah that's not even a name, but I'd

fuck her anyway, I don't care about the name."

"I just told you if anyone's fucking her it's me, and I kind of like her name"

"Do you think they gave her that name because of her eyes?"

"What, as a baby? I don't think so. She doesn't even look Chinese, she just has kind of cat eyes"

"Yep, the kind of cat eyes you want to look at while you're fucking her"

"I think you mean when I'm fucking her."

They continued down and down, chopping with their feet and sliding on hands, sometimes almost surfing down. Riding gravity down and down a dry slope extending like a reddish-brown cascade. The cliffs stretched either side for as far as one could see. It was as if the world had just collapsed along a long, jagged line, or a thick layer of dark bread had been ripped away roughly, revealing another, thousands of feet beneath. The difference in rock density coupled with the timeless rains had stripped away all earth beyond this hard volcanic ridge. The soils had been carried down by the same gravity and spread across the lower plains. It's true that it was some of the most fertile land on the continent, but the heat and humidity were unbearable. The local tribesmen were welcoming, hospitable, smiling, fine-looking. Both the men and women grew their hair in long curls, adorned with flowers either in little crowns or simply pushed behind their ears. The men would paint their eyes in a different fashion from the women. Though they were gentle and could have been perceived as soft-natured, they were formidable warriors. They wore traditional daggers and were adept at using them. But the heat! How they farmed and worked there was incomprehensible.

Beyond the plains was the sea. The snaking sea whose boiling marriage to the sun caused the fog and the rains that stripped back the land.

They stopped and surveyed their surroundings. They looked down and then back up. Below them the scene had hardly changed. They saw the same winding road and tan-brown sand and reddish rocks descending for as far as the eye could see. It's true that sometimes one could see the bottom but, in this case, it was barely visible. Looking up, we could see the top ridge from which we had started but it had telescoped away, far beyond easy reach. They were nowhere, they had barely dented this monstrous feat which they had glibly undertaken. It was getting to be late afternoon and they had probably been descending for three hours.

"Have you ever driven down there?"

"Well, not personally, but my uncle drove me down there once."

"How long did it take?"

"I don't know. About seven hours."

"Seven hours? By car? We're never going to get there today."

"We have to get back anyway, I have to eat something. I haven't eaten all day."

"Well, neither have I, no one has."

Now we started back up the slope. This time they were facing the wall of earth and rock. They used their hands and feet and the shoes that were full of reddish sand and tiny stones which had to be emptied every 20 minutes. It was much harder this way. There was no gravity to assist us. Their fine muscles were losing power.

"What are you going to eat tonight?"

"I don't know. Probably some kind of soup first, then some little salads and that beautiful stew that my mum makes. I know they made a load of different desserts."

"We should've brought water."

"We couldn't bring water, people would have thought we were going to drink it."

"What people? There's no one here! No one could've thought anything because no one is here."

"Yes, but if we'd walked out with a bottle of water people would've thought that."

"I fucking hate all this. It's so stupid."

"Don't talk to me about it, I didn't invent it."

"Do you think we're getting close? I'm getting really tired."

"Yeah, I guess we were using energy on the way down but you just didn't feel it. I can just about see the top."

"How long have we been climbing up?"

"I'm not sure, It seems like about two hours. We have to keep moving. We can't be here when it gets dark. It gets cold really fast. And there's all those monkeys."

"Oh fuck, I forgot about that. Do you think they'd attack us?"

"Well they've been known to take babies and children."

"Yeah, but we're not fucking babies. I'll just throw rocks at them."

"Yeah, if we see them, and there's loads of them. It's not just one or two."

"Well we're getting out of here anyway so it won't matter. I think I have to sit down for minute, I'm getting really tired."

"Yeah, all right, sit down for minute."

He sat and looked back out at the distant plateau. He was not as strong as me. He had a little layer of fat over his muscles. He could lift his own weight, and he did run fast. But it was easier for me to pull him up than vice versa.

"Are you ready to go?

"Yeah, I'm ready. Let's go."

We climbed on.
"I want to leave this town. Would you come with me? I'm gonna take my little brother with me."

"Where would you go?"

"France. We went to France once and it

was beautiful. Full of girls. I was only little but I remember it really well."

"Do you think we could drive there?"

"Yeah. I'm pretty sure, I have to look at a map."

"Yeah, OK. I mean they won't let us, but we could just do it, just need a car and passports. We could both drive. It would cost a lot in petrol but I can get money."

"Hey, I'm really sorry. I have to sit down again."

"No, that's OK, sit down if you need to sit down."

"We can't stay too long because it'll get dark. The sun is already really low."

"Yeah, of course. My legs are a little tired."

He was starting to look pale and his eyes

were dilating. We were not far from the top—maybe another hour and a half—but it was an hour and a half that we didn't have.

"OK, are you ready to go?"

"Yeah, lets go, but don't talk about food anymore, ha ha."

"Do you think we could live in France? I mean, you've been there, but I've never been anywhere but here. I know it feels like a prison sometimes but I think I'd want to come back here sometimes. Just to see my parents . . ."

We climbed for about another 40 minutes as the sun went down.

The mineral ore smell of the reddish soil. Our hands grazed, my legs are bruised, shoes filling with the red sand. I was beginning to feel tired and my legs and arms are heavy and weak and light at the same time. I could see the top.

"I have to stop."

"You can't stop, you can't stop now, we're nearly there."

"Yeah, that's what I mean. You go ahead and I'll just finish at my own speed."

"What do you mean?"

"You go ahead."

"No, I'm not going anywhere without you."

"I'll be OK."

"No you won't, you're not staying here alone."

"I really can't climb."

"Yes you can. You're just as strong as me and I can do it. Remember when you pulled me up a couple of weeks ago? You didn't think you could do it but you did it, remember?"

For the first time, I was scared. If he stays here, he'll freeze and those fucking gangs of baboons or whatever the fuck they are will be around. There's no way I'm letting him stay here. Maybe if we were two we could watch each other's backs, stand back to back and throw rocks at them. But he'll never make it like this.

"You can do it, we'll get back and have a big dinner. We're nearly there. I can't carry you, but you're gonna come."

"Take a deep breath and we'll start together."

"I can't do it yet."

"Yes, you can you're strong. Take a deep breath and start together."

"I can't do it yet."

"I'm not leaving you."

"Ok. I think I can do it."

We climbed slowly but steadily, and I stayed beside him, for he was like me and I couldn't imagine living without him. For another eternity we climbed in the passage from dusk to night. We didn't see animals though we knew they were near. We had stopped speaking altogether. We had neither eaten nor drunk for 15 hours. In this last effort, which seemed outside time but must only have been about 40 minutes, our legs shaking, we finally straightened with our backs to the abyss and stood upright, and saw the lights of the city.

PARIS 11ÈME

It runs with madness like the streams of water in its gutters. Hollow-eyed men engaged in deep conversation with invisible agents. Cracked women conceal the fissures of their minds with layers of makeup, the horror in their eyes brought further to life by the black frames they draw around them. This *gentrifugal* force has thrown out all of those who once lived, bought and sold there.

2ND ASCENT

"Well, that's all well and good but I still haven't seen him, I can't find him and it's been a long time. Too fucking long."

"You have to assemble a team. It's the only way you will find him, you need more coverage."

"A team? Of pilgrims?"

"Agents, pilgrims, whatever you call them. You need a team with specialist skills."

As I remember, when the team arrived at the site it was already night time. Pure bright moonlight, black and white powder world.

Disembarking from the small, silent transporter at a blind spot behind the giant auditorium. Although they themselves were hidden from sight they could clearly see a large white palace or temple far to their left perfectly lit. Its paneled domes appeared to be made from bone and to give off their own light like dust. They could have made them from bone, he thought, they certainly have the means.

"How did I get involved in this?"

"You have a particular skill needed for this operation. We all do."

He stared up at the hulking black door with studded plates that gave in to the space behind the wide shallow stage. This echoing space was lit only by the long shafts of light leaking from between the monolithic, canvas stage partitions.

The door looked immovable but proved surprisingly easy to open. It was so well enginecred that two people could pull it in its polished trench. It was probably designed thus so that a single strong bodyguard could open it to protect a member of the Royalty.

It is an auditorium and they are moving into the huge space behind the giant canvas screens of the stage.

On the stage is an actor or a perhaps a professor. He is telling anecdotes in a rich RADA voice. The audience is laughing and glowing in his stories and the warm golden light that escapes the stage. The audience is made up of young artists from rich families and this is their graduation. They have been chosen by the state to sit on these red velvet seats and that is why they are in this room.

At a quick pace and stooping, the other four members of the team run into the darkened space and position themselves and their bags of kit behind different partitions.

From her bag, the girl with the red hair brings out a box of six glasses and a large flask, and begins pouring a liquid.

James, meanwhile, produces something which resembles a garden light in the form of a foot-long nail. He holds it so that the steel tip is in the three-millimetre gap between the hard wooden floorboards. He turns the head one click to the left and it screws in, burrowing in like a tick and locking into position, sticking out of the floor. He clicks again and the device activates. There is no sound or light but I am conscious of a pulsing, possibly a sub-sonic, effect.

Now the professor, whom we will call Mr Simpson, has stopped his speech momentarily and Chloe, the girl with the red hair, still in her flight suit, steps onto the stage holding a tray of six drinks. From behind the stage I can see that they are faceted glasses like the Moroccan ones that we drank from as children, the ones with numbers on the bottom. Inside was a semi-clear liquid with what could have been a cherry inside but looked bigger. Almost like an egg yolk but bright red.

She hands one to the professor with a little bow.

Turning confidently to the audience, "Who would like to try a beautiful new cocktail? It's a natural recipe. You?"

(I found this woman beautiful. I'm fully aware of the subjective nature of this type of statement. The word 'find' is the important one here. How one finds someone beautiful or otherwise is the key. I realize there are many factors at play, many parameters. A friend once told me that if the brain were correctly stimulated, one could fall in romantic love with a dining chair in exactly the same manner).

There are about four thousand young adults in the auditorium and instead of being alarmed or surprised by this strange intrusion they are smiling and many of them are raising their hands.

Chloe is moving incredibly quickly and skillfully as Mr Simpson indicates with his eyes and little nods to whom the drinks should go. First to a bright-eyed girl in the sixth row. Then a handsome dark-haired young man at the back.

"Don't drink yet," says Mr Simpson, "wait to say 'cheers'."

As soon as the drinks are evenly distributed throughout the hall, Mr Simpson raises his own glass and sweeps the room with his gaze and then, in a deeper, dream tone: "to you all, Cheers!"

On hearing the word 'cheers', James turns the head of the device one more click and the pulsing stops.

Mr Simpson has a beatific smile on his face but he is leaning against the side of the lectern and slowly sliding down. Instantly, all those who have drunk the cocktail are slumped, smiling in their chairs. Instead of a crying out there is a strange sighing as the entire audience slowly slips into their chairs, immobile.

At this point I was horrified. "Why have we poisoned them?" I asked James. "What have you done? How did it work on everyone?"

"We haven't poisoned anybody. They're sleeping."

"How? Only a fraction of them drank it?"

"It's a mix of *entrainement* and suggestion. There is an isochronic effect. You felt the sub-sonic pulse, right? It's actually very good for you. They'll sleep and dream deeply.

They're expecting all of these artists to walk back through the city gates in exactly fourteen minutes. We have to leave now if we want to get inside the city walls. We have to start from inside. The outside is shielded."

Everyone is running quietly back out of the rear doors and round the building. It is becoming light now.

Now we are re-grouped in front of the great city doors. The other four, Luis, Chloe, James and Karine, are pulling combination suits from their packs. I have never seen suits like these. They are of a washed-out, greenish-grey and have copper-coloured, metallic foot covers and gloves. They have a wide strap around the upper torso with a small block at the back and a simple control unit positioned in the centre of the chest. It looked oddly like an old diving suit. Luis is helping me into mine and I lift my arms for him to adjust the straps.

"We need you to enter a code."

"What? What code? There are neither letters here nor numbers made of letters? There's no keypad?"

"Orion, by magnitude. You know it. It will be sufficient to do it in the air in front of you. We will do the rest."

"No seriously, there must be some device, a keypad???"

"We'll take care of that. Align yourself with the doors and give the code."

"With my hands?"

"Yes."

"In the air?"

"Yes."

Using the pattern of the simplest numeric

keypad I could remember, I place my hands in front of me in the positions of the stars in the constellation of Orion in order of magnitude. The others have slipped away. I try to do it as delicately as possible but am, nevertheless, standing alone gesticulating like a mad person before the great doors, maybe 40 metres in height. They also appear to be made of black iron but, unlike those of the theatre, these are immense.

As I place my hand in the final position the gargantuan doors begin to yawn open. A jagged, vertical line of dim light appears at the centre of the frame.

We are in.

"How did you use my gestures to open it?"

"We have a relayer that transmits to the lock. The frequency itself cost many lives to obtain."

Luis cranks the dial on my suit to the first setting, then his own, and I see him become blurred as the air around him, or perhaps the light itself, begins to oscillate.

"Now, run in!"

The great doors are now wide enough for a person to enter. Now two. Beyond it the grey pile of buildings and balconies begins almost immediately. It is steep but slopes back as if the entire waking city was a giant ziggurat. Bullets are now falling all around us as we run. Where are we going? I think to myself, we will be against those buildings in seconds, they'll rip us to shreds.

At about 50 metres, Luis's fuzzy arm slaps round against my chest and cranks the dial. There is a fizzing sound, a smell of negative ions and train sets and I feel all the metallic parts of the suit lock in spherical fields and lift into the air. We are falling upward and forward very close to the grey balconies with their iron railings.

"Is this Paris?"

"Yes, but it was rebuilt here by the dominions when the original became uninhabitable."

"Are we outside the Droom?"

No answer.

As we float up quickly we can see fractions of glimpses into the apartments. Children eating at little tables, coffee pots, biscottes, jam jars, couples in tee-shirts, televisions, little dogs, cereal packets ashtrays . . . All this blood that has been spilled, all those lives slowly choked. Each time we reach a roof another building starts a few metres back. And we continue.

"They won't fire towards the residents."

"Are we using them as shields?"

"No. They are programmed not to fire into civilian areas. We know that for certain. We'll be out of range soon."

Climbing on, rising, the other three in front in a loose triangle, me and Luis behind. The apartments become larger, the stonework more ornate, inside, the couples in robes and pyjamas, the residents and their furniture, older. Everything older.

The shooting dies off and we rise on.

"How does my suit know which way to go?"

"I've twinned it softly with mine. Do you want to try alone? It's fairly intuitive."

"Ok."

"Use the axis of the fields of your hands

to turn, curl your feet back gently to pull up, forward to descend. Like this."

He curled his legs softly back and we lifted away from buildings in our climb.

"Your hands can be relatively fluid but keep your elbows pointed in the direction you wish to go."

My body mimicked his movements as it had been doing the whole time without my knowledge. As he approached the vertical axis we perceived the fortress city stretching away in all directions and could no longer make out what was happening in the apartments.

"Are you ready to try?"

"Yeah, OK."

He turned the dial on his chest. "Be careful it's quite sensitive."
I felt cut loose, and was aware of the

wind in my face for the first time since the start of our ascent. As instructed, I gently arched back with my arms outstretched and, sure enough, found myself pulling away from the endless tower of apartments. I could see Luis shrink away in front of me as I pulled closer to vertical. Warily twisting the axis of my closed fists as if holding an invisible hoop, I began to spiral around my own centre of gravity. Sky and building rotating quickly around me until I put myself back in line, falling straight upwards. When the spinning stopped I was facing the wrong way and had to twist softly round through the rushing air until my belly was facing the vertical city again. Realising I was drifting far away from the others, I contracted my stomach muscles and pointed my fists at the khaki dots in the distance, this had the effect of plunging me back towards the balconies. I must have misjudged the speed of my approach because of the perspective. As I approached Luis I could tell I was going way too fast to match him by pulling up. As he was only about 15 metres from the buildings, I overshot him. Though I had managed to arch back enough to avoid a fatal impact, I was dragged violently upwards against railings, flower pots and stone until I fell into one of the balconies and lay pinned to the ceiling above it.

Panting heavily, struggling to pull myself back to the edge, I felt out of my depth for the first time. At a strange angle, with my back to the ceiling I realized I had badly bruised my left knee and wrist. What was I thinking? What the fuck am I doing here?

Using my good side to pull back round I was almost perpendicular, in line with the balcony, when I noticed it.

On the wall inside the apartment I noticed a painting of a Paris park bench with the familiar white, dusty sand and the pear cut-diamond shadows of the leaves on the dappled surfaces.

I know that painting. I could hear voices from inside also. There was a black framed poster of a concert, and a third of spectral, blue, balloon-like figures which I recognized also. The sounds of pigeons cooing, a formica table with a box of Italian chocolates on it and a Japanese mug of half-drunk coffee. There's a pistol on the marble mantle piece, a fat cat on the fold out sofa bed with reddish-white hairs on its black cushion.

What is this place? I'm staring frozen in anger and confusion at the contents of the flat. Voices I recognize inside, through the glass. They're waking.

The cat is staring angrily at me, ffffffvvvvvngg-ggggvvvvvvvffffffvvvv.

Maybe the cat? Made this sound? No it's the sound of my suit! How does it work?

I'm trying to study the dial on the chest plate when I hear a pang behind me. I turn my head towards it in time to see a pair of boot heels hanging down over the edge of the ceiling disappear.

For a second all I see is the sky, whiter and mistier then I remembered it. Then a gloved hand flies in, reaching for me. As soon as the head comes into view I see that it's Luis. Fighting to reach me.

"Don't touch the controls," he said, bracing himself with one knee against the ceiling, "don't look back in there, we have to get out of here right now."

When he felt he had purchase on my right arm he yanked me in two movements, first to the edge then, kicking away with his legs, clear of the balcony until we were falling upward again.

"I'm sorry, I just . . . lost control of it. I came too fast and the buildings just . . .

what is this place? Who's apartment was that?"

"It's my fault, I should have never let you try it alone. I'm going to get into some trouble for this."

Still holding my arm, he positioned me in a lock between his legs. Keeping his elbows facing forward in the direction we were flying, he adjusted the dial on his chest. I felt my suit react. "We're twinned again," he said. This time I succumbed completely to the movements, to the rushing air sound of the suits. He had said nothing in answer to my question. We were still flying close to the buildings but now I was desperate to see inside. In one apartment I could've sworn I saw the little dog waiting on a black vinyl sofa.

Somnolent God, where are you? Eyes turned away from your sons. Our most intrepid hearts extinguished!

What is this tower? The apartments are becoming larger, the architecture inspired by Inca and Egyptian forms now. There are rich, red and black carpets, bedrooms in ink-blue that have the aspect of burial chambers. There are no children in any of these apartments. I know that room. Above the bank, in the cottage, in mountain snow, miles from the nearest life, at the crossroads in the city by the . . .

We are now moving slow enough to see clearly that this façade is very much like the one we climbed together when it was the feast day and I was so hungry my legs wouldn't climb. The black, painted ironwork features look like they were designed in the 1920s. The mist is cool, I think these are clouds. The air seems thinner, very pure.

Now the apartments are made of jade, walls of lapis lazuli. Inside, one woman is wearing a grecian cotton dress. Her skin is a caramel brown and she has a pronounced bump in her nose. One apartment is made from pink coral and the woman who inhabits it has her hair in a braid like a crown on her head.

She is playing a strange black instrument. The sound is neither melancholy nor joyful but a terrible mix the two.

We are slowing. We see earth and a flat green plateau leading to the final apartment. It is a perfect stone rectangle in the golden proportions. The door that is cut into the side of it is a perfect upright rectangle. We are stopping on the seat threshold of this place. Luis is adjusting his control box and our toes and heels sink into the dry grass. We are not only no longer flying but the feeling is like walking on the beach after having swum for hours. The body feels its weight, a terrestrial, base object. One by one we enter this black opening. The inside is much like a small concert hall with a gilded back wall, and ink-blue ceiling with rows of starfish forms, forms representing stars and a stage at one end. There is no form on the stage, but there is a melody being played that sounds like a Babylonian festival song. The same melody can be found, sorry, heard, in some medieval dances from Brittany. Everything in this music is in threes. The stage is two rectangles, one horizontal and one vertical. The others walk cautiously towards it and pull themselves up onto the stage. They turn, indicating that I should join. The suit now seems heavy. The boots and gloves made of layers of metallic mesh require effort to raise.

I turn to face the perfect gold rectangle of the far wall, a sensation like liquid welling in the pit of my skull and beautiful waves of blue sensation sent down my spine. But there is no blinding light, no event to speak of. I realize, of course, that I'm a wholly uninteresting subject for reflection. Apart from the discretion of the reader (for which I am profoundly grateful), I am completely at the mercy of fate in all things.

"Take off the suits.We must remove all clothing here."

"What?"

Everyone is undressing and arranging their suits on the stage like bodies flattened out to two dimensions. Beneath the strange suits there were cream-coloured underwear longjohns which were also removed, folded very precisely and placed below the control boxes on the chests. Again I had no idea what I was doing and Luis continued to do the work of two, folding mine and then his. When was this rehearsed?

I have always been uncomfortable with public nakedness because my penis, although proportionally large for my body when hard, is fairly unimpressive in its dormant state. That by now my attention is turned towards the two girls may explain why I did not feel the usual pang of discomfort. Despite myself I cannot take my eyes off of the red-headed girl Chloe. She removes the last layer of utilitarian underwear and I am gazing. The cream colour of her skin with the reddish-brown curls of her pubic hair and beautiful contrast. She squats down to arrange the last of her clothes in the bag next to it to vertically. Her breasts are small and like perfect drops— droplets of wax on a candle. If they were tanned and freckled it would be acceptable also. If her hair was longer or blonde from the sun, if her skin was food for 1000 years I would not complain. Since I was a child I have always felt this way.

None of the pilgrims/agents show any reaction to their new state. It seems as if they have trained for it, as if they have spent hundreds of hours together like this. They have the same confidence naked as when fully clothed. I'm the only one who is affected. I also notice that since I entered this chamber my hands are more fleshy and the skin smoother and the bruises on my leg and wrist are no longer visible. I cannot see my reflection but, somehow, I know it, I am younger. Maybe as little as five years but still, younger. The little beauty spot at the base of my now hard penis has disappeared.

Everyone but myself and Chloe leaves through a dark, rectangular opening at the side of the elevated stage.

We are standing on the stone stage above the empty spaces in the suits where the heads are not. Closer, she is not smiling but says, "I'm glad you've chosen me." With her right hand outstretched to her side, first two fingers extended to the golden wall like a pistol, she reaches down between her legs with the fingers of her left, her palm flat against her reddish curls and cream skin. She moves the fingers of her right hand to her forehead and the left to my mouth. Fruit, food, spice, metallic flowers beam light spice, leather, star forms nourishing oblivion, hunger and peace. Arrival.

I don't know how long we fuck for but her eyes have two colours, a fragmented inner ring that is almost amber. Like a black hole in the centre of the horse head nebula.

For some reason the stone is not cold

One would expect the top of the Ziggurat to resemble a peak, smaller than its base, but no, as we emerge naked from the rectangle on the other side of this bunker-like structure we see something very different. The shale-coloured landscape is like a rolling ocean of small stones forming waves and craters. We are clearly at high altitude as the clouds are very close above our heads. Sometimes we find ourselves able to reach up and touch them and occasionally we find ourselves in the mist for a few seconds as the two membranes of dark blackish- grey stone and grey-white mist touch for a moment.

At high altitude one would expect the temperature to be cold or at least cool but this is not the case. The air is just below blood temperature with the illusion of coolness. There's so much space! To be naked in the mist but not cold . . . I don't understand. There is electricity in the cloud and one can feel it in the teeth like a subtle humming and in the perineum also.

The grey shale-like stone forms waves and lazy craters. We are all walking in this space between cloud and rock. Chloe stays nearest to me, and the others fanning out in front of us, their feet sometimes slipping on the top layer of rocks. James is the only one to have kept anything with him. He has a brown leather bag slung across his shoulder. He produces some kind of small reader similar to a dictaphone in size and shape. He seems excited as if he is finally living out some long held desire. I realize what this resembles the most. It is like the beach, a pebble beach which extends endlessly, rippling and undulating as if the beach were the calm ocean itself.

This is good, the conditions seem right. He's moving ahead of us to the ridge of a very large, shallow crater the size of a Ferris wheel on its side. He reaches again into his bag, this time producing a black pouch containing some kind of powder. Takes a handful of it.

"What's he doing?"

"He's trying to induce rain chemically."

James takes up the pose of a javelin thrower, his pale, naked shoulders flexed, his back diagonally bisected by the brown leather strap. Aiming into the air above the bowl. I feel a strange sensation of falling through myself, inwards.

He throws. As his hand passes his head and opens, there is a loud bang. A bolt of bluish-white flashes. Electricity is sucked into his hand and he is thrown about ten feet backwards across the flat, shaley pebbles. We run to him, our feet skating and slipping. He is burned on one side of his head, his hair is singed and his arm has little pieces of flesh missing. The holes are beginning to well up with blood. He is clearly winded and emitting a hissing, wheezing sound, his right eye looks strange.

"We have to get him back to the chamber, otherwise he'll be dead within a couple of hours."

"You'll have to continue alone. Don't worry, just remember your training."

You're close. You're close to me.

There are so many forgotten people in the upper corridors and tunnels of the Droom. Hunched in corners, slumped against the walls that lead to the transporter. Sometimes they choose a particular place for a reason known only to them and they remain there for long periods of time. What distinguishes one location from another? It's imperceptible to me but they are fiercely loyal to their place. I suppose that because they're either terribly lost or else they were never in true existence to begin with, it is a way of creating a meaning. It is hard to maintain the constant link with one's compassion. I'm sure that if there was more substance to me I would feel differently but I have been falling inwards for some time with no sign of a landmark. If only there was some thing onto which I could hook myself, or perhaps some plateau to break the constant descent. My hands look younger, folding in on the transporter there in the high mountain touching the mist, falling.

I've seen you all before, here and there.

What is this yearning? This beautiful emptiness? The bells that sound, superimposed like the expanding rings of drops falling in a puddle. The distant sound, like thousands of women ululating on a distant cliff? I think something terrible is about to happen.

3RD ASCENT

And then we saw the great procession snaking through the freshly cleaned streets. I think I should stay here and watch, it's only an instinct but I have a feeling he will pass if I stay here long enough. Distant horns sounding. We could not see the front of the procession as it was over the horizon, but from our vantage point up on the balcony above the bank (which is a launderette is a cottage on an island in that village in the heart of the old city) I could see its composition very clearly. the outer lines were made up of children wearing nothing but little cloths about their genitals but who were painted beautifully in one colour each. The colours were in a long sequence which included metals and oils and powders and lacquers and unfolded over the course of three days and restarted in a cycle. One had to be patient to observe the sequence but I had plenty of time. Eventually one could predict the next child's colour. I understood that the order was that of the dominant mineral compound in our star systems by order of magnitude. They were executing a kind of marching dance step in a count of six beats where they dragged a foot inward on the three, clapped on the four and did a little dip and a jump on the five and a half—six. Their timing wasn't perfect as it seemed they were not moving to the pulse we were hearing but by some more complex interference pattern. They were beautiful though and very touching to watch.

Just above their heads was a line of butterflies flying in a line. Most unusual! How does one train butterflies to fly in a line? Again, their colours changed gradually as they were arranged by species.

Then came waves of men and women in the uniforms of their trades. The next row was composed mainly of mechanical creatures with their bare wires and whirring cogs visible. These machines were made of exotic woods and noble metals.

Behind them were not individual creatures but multitudinous black wooden rippling beings. They formed a stretched mountain or centipede and were in constant coupling with themselves. They had layers of pink

velvet pinched in folds between their
ornate chrome plates and black panels.
Smooth rods passed smoothly in and
out of their rubber apertures.

In the centre of the advancing column
were chariots. Giant wooden structures
carved with gods and dripping with
ornament, animals of many kinds, copulating bodies in extraordinary positions,
grimacing black-faced demons with red
coronas of horns, golden teeth and eyes
like the flesh of white fruits holding

shining black seeds within. Behind thin veils, priests could be seen. They were pulled by magnificent elephants in teams of four. Their giant wheels rimmed with iron hoops and their spokes like vases, each hewn from a single tree.

Those present were not passive observers but participants in this. Men with baskets on their heads passed through the gathered crowd. Piles of crimson fruits resembling human hearts, peeled and dripping with inky-red juice were piled up in the baskets and changing hands. The pilgrims bought these with dull-looking coins that may well have been nickel or tin. They held them in their upturned hands awaiting the signal.

Suddenly a trumpet sounded two short blasts and one long one.

A roar went up from the crowd and the air was filled with arcs of fruit and spraying red juice. The sky darkened with what appeared to be a hail of human hearts, directed at the monks lurching in the turrets of the wooden castles perched high on the chariots.

The ritual clearly had its origins in the offering of these fruits to the gods but had transformed over the millennia into a type of sentimental food fight

She looked up at the turret of one of the chariots: "It's him! He's in there!"

"Impossible, no way."

"I must must try to reach him, to warn him." In a split second she had decided.

She pushed away from the balcony, turning and sprinted towards the stairs. By the time anyone had taken stock of the situation, she had thrown herself down the black metal stairs behind the building disappearing from view.

Past the coffee shops and the estate agents and the betting shops. Pushing through the crowd, spat out into the space at the edge of the vast snaking procession.

I have no choice. If I'm to catch him I must act now.

All but hurdling the line of children, two of them, one cobalt blue and one a strange ferrous menstrual blood colour are knocked over. The next ones stopping to see what was wrong. The line of butterflies is still unbroken but lines of exotic birds are breached. Giraffes in gilded harnesses thrown out of step and lurch around. Wheel chairs containing giant putrid-smelling flowers pushed by giant matrons are shoved aside. On and on through lines of moss-covered tanks now spattered with crimson, a phalanx of the dead. Teachers, workers from the shirt factory, cartographers, wheelwrights, tailors and pill makers all parted as I shoved my way across the lines, cutting a diagonal tooth into the lines, to the foot of the copulating wooden machine. Although I barely had time to breathe or examine my surroundings I had a thought. How banal the dead are when seen up close. Transport workers, milliners, waiters, banker's clerks and their like. Distance had rendered them glamorous but with proximity one is struck by their ordinariness. I stared up, early evening sky streaked with red. The central column of chariots is beyond this one. I must scale it.

The machine is moving, crawling inexorably forward, emitting strange yearning sighing sounds. It is like a stretched pyramid, of moving wood and chrome parts now spattered with the rain of crimson juice and the heart-shaped fruits themselves. I started to climb, grabbing at piston-like limbs that writhed and pushed at different rhythms. Each time I wished to find a new grip or foothold I had to check that the hand or foot in question would not be crushed by the crossing of the limbs or against the body of the machine. The wooden rods made wheezing, sucking sounds as they entered the black and pink rubber openings. I climbed on. It was treacherous going. A footresting on a wooden piston, a hand hooked into a black rubber mouth and all the time in motion. The rain of juice became more steady and the fruits fell all around with increasing frequency. As I reached my left hand to grab hold of an undulating ridge of large ebony tongues, a fruit landed on them and split with a squelching sound.

But, it looks . . . it can't be . . . there is the left ventricle, I recognize it. I become aware of distant drums and rhythmic sounds emanating from the bowels of the machine. I feel weak but there is no option but to hang on, I'm much too high to fall. Taking a great risk, I cling on to a moving and slippery shaft with my right hand and try to reach for the

the nearest fruit. It's as I thought, it's split but the tips of my fingers feel that there are the holes where the arteries should be. I looked around. There are others falling close by all the time.

The sky is darkening and I am much more conscious of beating drums, horns, chanting voices. Keep climbing, hope that the chariots are still moving at the same rate as the machine otherwise all this will be in vain. It is harder to grip the moving parts and sometimes my foot has barely found purchase when it slips off some strange limb and my hands tighten in terror. It takes me some moments of panting and murmuring each time to convince my shaking limbs to climb on. The groaning, sighing machine is becoming more agitated. An object hits me in the leg, I do not look, I know what it must be. Climb on. The lush pink velvet cinched and bunched into ornate apertures is now soaked with juice.

I'm not far. If I summon a last push I can reach the peak and I should be near him. Everything is running with blood and humming low. I realize I'm crying. There are tears. Not a human crying but an animal crying like the friction of stones deep in the earth. This is it, the last day of climbing. The sky is dark, fruits hit me from all angles, they are bunching up in the hollows of the moving limbs and building up in drifts on every surface. I can hear the growling of the little dog, the beating of some type of gong deep in the machine, the clashing of cymbals,

"Don't you think you have undertaken something that is beyond your capabilities?"

"Yes, I admit it. I'm thirsty, I've been climbing for days now."

"It has also been raining for days hasn't it?"

"Raining? No . . . you mean . . . the . . . no!"

"Yes, there's no harm, no one will think less of you."

In all the up-facing cavities and concave parts of the machine are pools of juice, but it is mixed with pieces of fruit and the thick, waxy grease that lubricates the machine's movements.

"No one will judge you. You are soaking in it anyway. It has run down your hair and into your mouth, your breasts. Everything is sticky with it. You've already tasted it."

"I don't want to be part of this."

"You are part of this."

"I'm so thirsty."

I arrange myself in the most stable position I can near a pool that seems reachable. There is a hole right behind it and a wooden bar the diameter of a small tree trunk comes out of that hole into a kind of bowl at regular intervals. I wait to see the pattern. It appears every 30 counts and pumps into the cavity furiously then disappears for 1 . . . 2 . . . 3 . . . 4 . . . and again. About a count of 4.

I wait for it to stop. My left hand is secure but the wooden ridge on which my feet are planted is moving and slippery. As the rod disappears, I lean across with one cupped hand and steal what I can like a humming bird. But by the time it gets back to my mouth there's barely a mouthful. It is salty and sweet and has a metallic, thick fruit taste but it's effect is almost instant. It's good. I'm so eager to fill my hand again that I forget to count well and have to snatch my hand from the path of the rod.

I get nothing.

Wait. Next time I count and remove my hand at exactly the right moment but have less than I wanted when it reaches my mouth.

Also there is a chewy piece of something in there that I swallow down with the juice. I feel better.

"Doesn't that feel better now? You're nearly there."

The sky is black, apart from the fireworks and the moon, on the day in the third month of the year when I finally pull myself to the top. I'm not the same person I was when I started the climb.

About three and a half weeks had passed when I finally hauled myself to the top. It was very difficult to gauge the passage of time because the sky was in constant darkness but one could tell roughly when night had come because of the drop in the frequency of the fruits falling all around. It's true that I felt guilty having fed on them, knowing full well their provenance, my hands had become caked with it and except for the palms which looked pallid, everything was caked and matted with semi-dried blood. My forearms were tingling and seemed to be laughing with pain. The contrast between inside and outside of my hands, the line down the outer edges of my thumb and forefinger where the caked red met the sickly white was like the day and the night, I mean to say in another time where those things contrasted.

But I was upright on the peak of this long, snaking mountain. I had slept on any moving part wide and stable enough to hold me. Sometimes I had caught what I could draped over a moving rod like a shirt on a washing line. Now I was at the summit my heart pounded to see. I was able from this vantage point to see everything about me to all points of the compass. I could see the little apartment which is above the cottage above the bank in the mountains in the heart of the city. I could see the South Downs, the Grand Rex, and, in the distance, I could see the cliff sloping down towards the boiling sea. As I had hoped, the wooden chariot was almost within reach.

He's there! He hasn't seen me. I shout but the ululating and blowing of horns, the cluttering of the ceremonial cymbals are already saturating the thin, warm air. I try again. The wind blows the sound back into my mouth. A few metres and a thin cream gauze are the only thing that separates us. I have to jump. There's no run up, only a few feet. I have no choice. It's thousands of feet down, it would take seven hours by car! I don't care. I have to do it now. Without further thought I took two steps back and jumped with all my force for I had nothing to lose. The fruit must have nourished me and I met the edge of the turret harder than I had foreseen.

Pulling my leg over the wooden railing, pulling aside the gauze I could see that it was not him. The occupants were not real humans but wooden simulacra like those in the little diorama, painted and lacquered in such a way that they appeared to be brushed with honey. How could I have believed this? The figures wobbled slightly in their fixings which gave some illusion of movement. It's true that the craftsmanship and painting of the effigies was slightly crude but it was this abstracted element coupled with the misting of the gauze that had rendered them so perfectly real from a distance.

"Where are they?"

"The priests?"

"Yes, the fucking priests and where is he?"

"There have been no real priests in these turrets for many generations. They have all departed on the pilgrimage."

I let out a howl of despair, like stones grinding deep underground producing friction sound, but . . . not human sadness, normal human crying into the deep animal. My eyes well and I vomit a stream projection of red blood off the balcony and collapse with my head against the carved wooden bars.

"It's OK. Try to get some rest. try and sleep a little."

We are like parasites feeding on time. Light is food for the eye and thus there are lights that taste of fruit. Light is the food of the eye but darkness is its wine.

"How long do I have to stay here?"

"Do you mean how often does the gateway open? It's like the story of the floating hoop and the sea turtle. One could look down into the dark waters for such a very long time. Sometimes miracle phenomena do occur. Shoals of phosphorescent fish, illuminated from within, pink mist at dawn. And yes, one day, as you gaze through that circular gate, that portal eye, you will see the form of the turtle looming from the void, swimming directly towards you from the depths. There will be fear of course and many times he will appear to be in line but as he nears, your heart will break as you realize that he is not aligned with the hoop. This is the hardest moment as you know that he will be gone another thousand years. But yes, in the end, one day, the gate will open."

I am now running back towards the apartment above the bank above the dry cleaners in the cottage in the snow in that old house by the dry hill in that desert town.

It is more like flying in a dream

Only the little dog is with me.

As the little dog turned the final corner he could see the approach to the hill, the bottom of which was already thronged with people. The entire approach to the crossroads would be extremely busy and although the streets had been redesigned and rebuilt numerous times, the risk of accidents was never far away. It would take only a moment of panic and the people would run, pushing, jostling and finally trampling each other to try to reach an imaginary safety. The apprehension of this blood rite would make the twitchy, horse nature of the human animals like raw nerves. Executions are normally held on Thursdays or Fridays.

Working his way through the crowd, he arrived at the crossroads and the perimeter which was marked out by policemen in blue shirtsleeves and berets. Over white,

sandy, cotton-covered shoulders he could
see the three condemned men at about
fifty metres. With their heads hung down
he could not really make out their faces
but they were not at all as he had ex-
pected them to look. The three criminals
looked too young. They were barely old
enough to drive. Not old enough to be
fathers. They were disheveled and with
their unkempt, patchy beards, kneeling
about five metres apart. Tiny mists from
their mouths and nostrils. They were all
three dressed in white tee-shirts with
circles resembling a target approximately
above the heart. I don't understand, he
thought to himself, those shirts are
reserved for firing squads, but there are
no posts. Why are they kneeling? They
must be freezing there. Marc felt such
terrible pity and fascination. The main
purpose of these events seemed to be to
create a transference, a distance. He
fought the thoughts that were being
projected into the minds of the gathered
pilgrims: it's not me, those people are

not me. Thank god it's not me. No, he thought, they are me, that could be me, worn out and broken, pissing myself. Still begging, still murmuring to no one that I had done nothing wrong. Waiting like a slumped sack for the end.

And then he thought, give them some clothes, you bastards, it's too cold.

From the only breach in the crowd three men appeared, two dressed in white, one in a black combination.

Taking positions to the right of the three shabby victims, one of them read a ceremonial passage from a red and gold book, then began with a formal notice, listing the crimes of the condemned. They were suitably pathetic reasons: cutting short the ceremonial strings on a holy day, consorting with animals (namely a small dog), reciting forbidden poems, evoking the names of parishads of enemy states.

Even though the list of mediocre violations was short, it seemed to extend for an unusually long time.

Finally, the man in black whose face was covered turned to his accomplice who held out a wooden box. He opened it to reveal a bright metal blade like a long question mark in a pit of green velvet. It looked heavy and ornate. A beautiful object.

Marc recognized it instantly as the one he had sharpened in the Droom all those years ago.

How can it be? How did they get their hands on it? This means I am part of it!

The man in black held the weapon downward with the curved inner edge forward and walked quickly to the side of the first prisoner. He gave him a tap on the back with the side of the blade and he raised his head a little.

In that instant which stretched out, Marc recognized him and froze. It was Mr Simpson. It was him many years ago when he was young but it was him alright. How had they managed to capture him?

Does that mean . . . the other two must be Cutmond and Luis, the young Spaniard . . . no this cannot be . . . no, no, no. Cutmond is a foul beast but I don't wish him this . . . no, this is wrong . . . take me instead . . . no . . . no, please, Mr Simpson is a kind man.

His tears were streaming, no, you can't do it . . . you must not do it. No no no he was one of the only ones who was ever kind to me . . . no no . . . take me instead.

The man gave a second harder tap on Mr Simpson's back at a particular point on the spine and he extended his neck as a reflex. With a swift oval motion he swung the blade over his head and dropped it perfectly into the pale, exposed flesh below his head removing it instantly.

The flood, the spraying of dark crimson life simply didn't happen. Yes, the body slumped forward and the head rolled in a little semi-circle but there was no blood to be seen. What's more, instead of lying awkwardly on its cheek on the cold tarmac, the head somehow rolled cheekily onto what was left of its neck and looked around.

The tears were still wet on Marc's cheeks but his mind was now burning. What was this? Why? The only reference he had for such a turn of events was the stories of the local sorcerers in Burgundy who could stop a stuck pig from bleeding by reciting from a book. He had never actually seen it.

The executioner looked bemused, tilted his head to the side.

He turned to the man bearing the box
and gestured groundwards at the head.

The crowd was silent.

Handing the box to his colleague, he
strode quickly to the severed head which
was still looking around nonchalantly.
Simultaneously, the executioner moved
to the second prisoner, who, when tapped
with the sword, revealed himself indeed
to be Cutmond. He had such a terrified
schoolboy look on his face that it was hard
to imagine he had been the architect of
so much misery. I felt deeply sorry for him.

The official in white grabbed Mr Simpson
by the hair to lift his head but it would
not move. It was not so much heavy as
seemingly welded to the ground. At
this the crowd gasped. The young Mr
Simpson raised his eyebrows. And tried
to look up at him. There are accounts of
heads remaining conscious for minutes
after decapitation I thought, still. He put

his back into it but only succeeded in slipping and accidentally kneeling for a second in front of the head. He gestured to the third official who took a second to register the command, before passing the book and the wooden box to the nearest police man. He trotted over to help.

As the two men strained, the executioner, visibly perturbed by the unusual events, looked back and forth from the activity behind him, then to the crowd which was now murmuring. Finally, as if a lock had been released, the head rose in their hands causing them to stumble backwards. They regained their balance and although it clearly had the weight of a normal human head, they carried it back with as much dignity as they could summon, placing it by the body of its former owner

In order to maintain the momentum, the executioner took the decision to continue his work as pre-ordained.

Again the same method, a sharp tap on the spine causing the neck to flex and the arcing blade came down in practiced perfection removing the head. This time there was liquid. Gushing arterial spurts of velvet, at once horrifying and instantly corresponding to the scene that all had pictured in their heads. However, after a few seconds it became clear that the gathering had been so distracted that they hadn't noticed that the liquid was in fact a velvety *green* colour. At first they presumed it was a trick of the light. But suddenly the crowd started to emit howls of terror as it dawned on them.

Then, suddenly, a harrowing scream from the crowd as attention returned to the first prisoner. The head, which had just been retrieved and balanced upright, toppled over and rolled back onto its neck. The now reunited body-head straightened upright.

"Please don't kill me, I'll be good, I am good," said Mr Simpson in his plummy accent. He lifted his head, now confidently resting on his body. The sarcasm in his voice was clear and he seemed to wink at the crowd. "Please, I promise, I'll be such a good boy."

"You fucking idiots," came Cutmond's voice, "you fucking plebs, hahaha!"

But there was no sign of him. Only a large, green, sparkling puddle with a white tee-shirt soaking in it from which a tiny field mouse pattered into the crowd.

The executioner sank to his knees.

Mr Simpson stood up to screams from the crowd and it was clear that neither he nor the young Spaniard were tied or restrained in any way.

"Oh, please, please I'll be such a good boy, do you see? Do you understand

now?" And with that, he and Luis walked
through the same breach from which
the officials had entered.

His neck is a tube
His head is a box
He is the smartest of all the robots

"We are delighted to announce that
today's execution is cancelled and in its
place there will be a musical interlude
by the magical entity Lata Mangeshkar.
The liquid drums and eternal ornaments
of this star's voice will delight you. Feel
free to dance. There are no restrictions.
Today has been declared a nationwide
amnesty."

—Good morning, afternoon, night.
Which do you perceive it to be?

—I perceive it to be morning

—Then, good morning. I am not cleared
to discuss how this has come about. We

found your file when we burned across the network, that's why I was assigned to you.

You were clearly a perfect candidate. No root, no anchor, no connection to any place. Not to a town, not to a tribe, and by the time you were 17, not even to a dimension.

The ideal profile.

In normal cases, the role requires total obedience but in yours it was not necessary.

The report includes two different scenarios. Both witnesses claim to have seen you slumped against a wall in the late afternoon near your apartment. Your consciousness seems to have been trapped in what you call the Droom.

—Now that I think about it, it is conceivable that the door codes were laid out as constellations as seen from the northern hemisphere. The order of the numbers being the sizes or magnitudes of the stars. In this manner the door to the escape pod, the little one-room studio you keep in case there is an accident on the crossing, are, respectively, the Southern Cross and Andromeda.

—That's absolutely correct, you're very observant. By this means, if one is familiar with the entire night sky one can have access to any apartment in Paris. Or London for that matter. That is why you were unable to read the codes on the door above the bank. Because there was no logic to them. They were neither letters nor numbers made of letters.

—So does this mean one has to memorize all the stars in the night sky?

—Not necessarily, one only has to memorize those constellations to which one is likely to travel. Those which

contain twinned particles or worlds
accessible by the Droom.

When one returns from deep space it's
normal to want to warm the hands and
feet. Luckily, the escape pod has an
airlock which naturally holds some heat.
The streets of Paris are often cold.

I once worshipped before fire, bears, the
sun. Now I worship only before mystery.
I have receded as far into myself as
possible, there is no farther and, yet, he
still hasn't made his appearance. I hang
like a languorous chord on the air. I have
no contact from my friends or loved ones.

—Listen extremely carefully. Although
I'm not cleared for refuge, I will now
give you the dissolution code for the
Droom, for we now consider that you
have given and rendered fully. You
were actually quite brave in the face of
it. You were the elder, you were the
benevolent voices, you are the love of,

you are both the woman seeking and
the man and search, you are the search
you are. You now hear yourself, you
now can translate the voice of the little
dog. Although you have heard the
phrase for before, the trigger phrase,
The sound key that will dissolve all but
the mouth of the sun all but the tiny
flame that feels fills all time.

A concert where the conductor is playing
out the constellations in order of
magnitude.

The End

poetry titles from The Onslaught Press

haiku titles